Dancing Princess

Even though I had no idea why these people were watching us, I'd told myself that they'd never pick me in a billion years. Then for a second it had looked as though I was in with a teeny chance, and a little firework had exploded in my stomach. But when I'd heard those words about how I'm not flexible enough, the sparks from the firework had burned me inside and made my throat sting.

Ballerina Dreams

Collect all the books in the series:

Poppy's Secret Wish

Jasmine's Lucky Star

Rose's Big Decision

Dancing with the Stars

Dancing For Ever

Ballerina Dreams

Dancing Princess

Ann Bryant

The publisher would like to thank Sara Matthews of the Central School of Ballet for her assistance.

First published in the UK in 2005 by Usborne Publishing Ltd,
Usborne House, 83-85 Saffron Hill, London EC1N 8RT, England.
www.usborne.com

Cover photograph by Ray Moller.
Illustrations by Tim Benton.

A CPI catalogue record for this title is available from the British Library.

JFMAMJJAS ND/05
ISBN 0 7460 6433 0

Printed in Great Britain.

1 The Visitors

Hi, I'm Poppy. Right now I'm in class at the Coralie Charlton School of Ballet and I'm a bit jittery. Actually, I'm always nervous in class. Well, *semi*-nervous and *semi*-excited. Mum says it's the adrenaline whizzing round my body. I think she's right. Only the whizzing is more of a buzzing because doing ballet gives me the best buzz in the whole world. In fact, if ever I couldn't dance for any reason, I wouldn't feel like living.

This is my favourite part of the lesson, the *port de bras*, which you pronounce *porderbra*, because all ballet terms are in French. The music for this exercise makes my arms feel like silk scarves floating in the breeze. When I practise at home it's never the same in the silence or with different music.

All the girls in my class are really good at ballet. I mean, they're better than me. If I said that to my best friends Jasmine and Rose they'd both tell me I was talking rubbish. Jasmine would go on about how expressive my dancing is and as for Rose, well I can just see her standing there with her hands on her hips giving me one of her *dur* looks... *So how come you're in grade five then?* I know she'd be right in one way. But I do have to work very hard to keep up with everyone else, partly because Jasmine and I are easily the youngest in the class, and I'm even a bit younger than Jasmine.

You should see Miss Coralie. She looks beautiful today. It's not just her swirly black skirt or her tight white top – it's her face. I don't think she's got any make-up on but she still looks beautiful with her dark hair and her glowing skin. Her eyes are big and browny green. I've no idea how long her hair is because it's always in a tight bun. I wonder if she *ever* wears it loose.

"Let's try that *arabesque* again, girls. Other arm, Sophie. I shouldn't have to say that at this level."

That's another thing about Miss Coralie. As well as being beautiful, she's also very very strict. I felt sorry for Sophie. If that had been me I would have gone red and my heart would have started popping, which is what it always does when I get really nervous or worried.

I stretched the foot of my raised leg and the knee of the supporting leg as hard as I could and tried not to wobble. My whole body was aching from holding the position for so long. Miss Coralie was right in front of me now, walking along the line to check us individually.

"Lift up out of your ribs, Poppy... That's right." She moved on to the next person so I was allowed to lower my leg and close. If you've never done ballet, all I can say is that the relief of standing back in fifth position, after all that balancing and trying to make every bit of your body hold a perfect position, is as big as the relief you feel when you've been bursting for the loo for the last hour and you finally get to go.

"Let's do some *pirouettes*. Fifth position."

Mrs. Marsden, the pianist, flipped her page over and then the whole room went silent because there was a knock at the door. That might not seem particularly unusual, but I can assure you, it *is*. You see, no one *ever* interrupts one of Miss Coralie's classes. My eyes went straight to her face expecting to see a big furious frown.

"*Ah*, that will be our visitors." And she glided over to open the door.

I couldn't believe it. Why wasn't she cross?

Everyone in the class looked round with puzzled, shocked expressions. Jasmine let out a little gasp. Her eyes were even wider and darker than normal. Mrs. Marsden was wearing a welcoming smile and didn't seem the least bit surprised.

A moment later, in walked a lady wearing a dark blue suit, and a man in a black one. I could hear them talking in low voices, apologizing for interrupting. Miss Coralie just smiled and led them to two chairs at the front.

"They must be important," Jasmine mouthed to me.

That's what I'd just been thinking and I guessed everyone else had too because we all went back to our fifth positions and stood there like tall, straight ballet statues.

"Right girls, let's get on."

And we were straight back doing *pirouettes* as though nothing had happened. Miss Coralie didn't even introduce the visitors, which made me more curious than ever about them.

For *pirouettes* you have to spot. That means you fix your eyes on something at the front and when you spin round you whip your head round at the last moment and fix your eyes straight back on your spot. I could feel without even looking that Tamsyn was doing brilliant *pirouettes* beside me, never losing her balance once. She loves it when there's an audience – even an audience of two. It makes her dance better.

"They must be talent scouts," I heard Immy say quietly to Lottie when we'd finished the *pirouettes* and Miss Coralie was having a quick word with Mrs. Marsden.

"Why? What for?" asked Tamsyn in slightly more than a whisper.

But Immy couldn't answer because Miss Coralie was ready to carry on. "I'm going to build the *relevés* into a sequence," she said.

We all stood up two centimetres straighter and my body stiffened as though I'd got armour on the inside. Trying to remember steps in a sequence is my worst thing and I always have to concentrate extra hard for this bit. But how could I, when my brain space was being totally used up by wondering about the two visitors? I couldn't keep my eyes off them. It was as though I might find some clues in their faces or written on their clothes about who they were and what they were doing here.

They watched us like hawks the whole time, and occasionally one whispered into the other one's ear. It made me so nervous I felt like lying down and taking deep breaths. *Just calm down, Poppy,* I told myself fiercely. *They're not going to choose you, whoever they are, are they?* And I knew the answer was: *No, they're not.* After all, there are lots of others in the class with better technique than me – Tamsyn and Jasmine, for a start. And then there are the ones who are more flexible than me – Tamsyn again, and Isobel and Beth... And as for the ones with a good memory for sequences, well that's just about everyone except me...

No, there was only one reason why I might be chosen and that was if they happened to be looking for someone with red hair. But what a stupid reason to be picked out by talent scouts. It would mean that they weren't even talent scouts – they were hair scouts.

"Right, let's try it through, all together first and then we'll do it a row at a time."

My heart popped so loudly I thought everyone must have heard. And my eyes flew open because I'd just realized I hadn't been listening to a single word Miss Coralie had been saying. I'd been in my own little dream world. Now I was going to look a complete idiot because I wouldn't be able to do the steps. My only hope was to watch the two rows in front of mine as hard I could and try to pick it up from them. Then I'd get another chance to watch them when we did it a row at a time.

I could feel my face reddening as we went through it all together, and it was obvious I was the only one who didn't have a clue because I was always one step behind.

And Miss Coralie had noticed too. "Poppy, are you on another planet today?"

She was giving me a half smile, but if the visitors hadn't been there she wouldn't have smiled at all.

I marked the sequence through with my hands while the first two rows had their turns, but I knew I hadn't completely got it.

"Right, third row... *Preparation*...and *one* and *two* and *stretch* and *two* and *use* your *eyes* and *open* your *shoul*ders...*one* and *two* and *nice* work *Jas*mine, *good* and *two* and *fin*ish *there.*"

I'd managed to get through it all right and I'd tried my hardest to use my eyes and dance expressively, but I knew I hadn't done all the steps properly. Jasmine had done it really well though. I hadn't had time to watch her of course, but I could just feel how perfectly on the beat she was. Jasmine's got the fastest brain ever. She's so lucky.

While the last row was doing the sequence I watched the visitors. They were whispering about Tamsyn, and Tamsyn knew it. She was doing flexing exercises at the *barre*. She never does that right in the middle of class. It was obvious she wanted to show the visitors how supple she is. The lady reached into her handbag and took out a notepad and wrote something down.

Then when we were getting back in our rows I saw them looking at Jasmine. *Good*, I thought. I mean, I know Tamsyn's a really good dancer and definitely the most flexible in this class, but it really annoys me when she shows off so much. The lady was writing in her pad again. I hoped it was about Jasmine. After the *relevé* exercise we went over the sequence we did last week. I love this part of the lesson because I always practise really hard between lessons to make sure that I can do the sequence perfectly – well, as perfectly as possible for me – the second time round, and if I can't remember it properly, Jasmine helps me.

We did it a row at a time and I didn't feel even the tiniest bit nervous any more because I'd realized something obvious. The visitors couldn't be looking for a girl with red hair. Otherwise, they would have picked me straight away and then gone home. And they definitely wouldn't choose me for any other reason because there were so many better girls to choose, so I might as well stop feeling anxious and tense and just dance.

When it came to the third row I stood up straight in my starting position. The music reminded me of big billowy clouds racing across the sky. I tried to make my dancing big too, springing up high on the *soubresauts* and opening my arms wide to match the music. And when it finished I wanted to do it all over again the feeling was so magical and wonderful.

"Nice, Poppy!" said Miss Coralie.

And that made the feeling even better because Miss Coralie hardly ever gives compliments. All the same, I knew the visitors wouldn't be interested in me. Fancy watching on a day when I'd got Tamsyn on one side and Jasmine on the other. I could have sprung as high as a flea with pointy toes like a sharpened-up pencil, and *still* no one would notice me between those two brilliant girls.

At the end, Miss Coralie told the whole row that it was lovely and we all went off to the sides to watch the last row doing it. I was quite near the front and I got a big shock because the visitors were looking at me. I hadn't imagined it, I was sure. I quickly looked away, but not before I'd seen the lady write something in her notepad, and a moment later I heard her whisper to the man, "...not flexible enough, I'm afraid." And the man replied, "No, you're right."

Even though I had no idea why these people were watching us, I'd told myself that they'd never pick me in a billion years. Then for a second it had looked as though I was in with a teeny chance, and a little firework had exploded in my stomach. But when I'd heard those words about how I'm not flexible enough, the sparks from the firework had burned me inside and made my throat sting.

2 An Important Decision

At the end of class we did the *révérence* and then went out.

"Did they put you off?" I asked Jasmine quietly when we were in the changing room.

She nodded. "A bit."

"Well, you shouldn't let them put you off," said Tamsyn in her loud voice. "If you're a dancer you should expect people to watch you and it shouldn't affect you one jot...except to make you dance even better."

"It's all right for you, you're so brilliant!" said Lottie.

"Yeah, they were watching you the whole time," said Immy.

"Really?" Tamsyn looked round at everyone, pretending to be surprised. "Were they? I didn't notice!"

Jasmine and I exchanged a look.

"Anyway, I heard them asking Miss Coralie if they could come back next week," said Sophie, "so they can't have decided on anyone yet."

Tamsyn's face clouded over then, and Jasmine gave me another look, this time with wide eyes. I smiled at her, but neither of us said a word because we both knew that the moment we got out of the building we'd start talking nineteen to the dozen, as my mum would say, about everything that had happened. I put my ballet things into my bag and thought how lucky Jasmine was. She was in with a good chance of being picked. If I were her I'd rush home and practise solidly all week long to make myself as flexible as Tamsyn. After all,

Jasmine was just as good as Tamsyn in every other way.

And as I had that thought, it turned into a much bigger one. Why didn't *I* rush home and practise all week long? If I really pushed myself, maybe I could make a difference to my flexibility by the next lesson. But then I turned round to see if Jasmine was ready to go, and there was Tamsyn, sitting on the floor with her legs practically in the sideways splits and her top half leaning forwards so she could write down her new mobile number for Immy and Lottie. Her back was nearly parallel with the ground she's so supple. And I just knew that there was no point in me stretching like mad all week. No point at all. I'd never be able to do that in a million years, let alone a week.

"Are you ready, Poppy?" asked Jasmine.

I nodded and started to follow her with heavy legs and an even heavier heart.

*

An Important Decision

The next day at school I met up with Rose at the beginning of morning break, as usual. She came flying out of the Year Six door with her hair streaming all over the place.

"Hi! Did you have visitors in your class at ballet?"

"Yes! Did you?"

"Oops! I'm forgetting the golden rule!" She grabbed my hand and started dragging me off to the far corner of the playground. "No ballet talk in front of boys."

Once we were completely alone, we couldn't stop gabbling. It was just like a repeat of Jasmine and me after class yesterday. Jasmine doesn't go to the same school as me and Rose, but we're still all best friends together. We call ourselves the triplegang.

Rose seemed to be as excited as I was. "They looked at me quite often, but goodness knows why when I'm such a beginner!"

"You're not a beginner any more, Rose. Just

because you joined later than anyone else…"

"By about five years!"

"Yes, but you were good enough to go straight into grade four and you've caught up loads and loads…"

"I'm not good enough to go up into grade five with you and Jazz though."

"But you're so flexible…"

"*That's* not a big enough reason to be chosen, is it?"

"But still…if they were looking at you…"

"I *think* they were." She screwed up her face as though she were trying to remember precisely what had happened, then suddenly looked back at me with big bright eyes. "What do you think they need dancers for anyway?"

"I don't know."

"Did they whisper to each other in your class?"

A big sigh stopped me from answering, as I remembered the lady's words… *Not flexible enough, I'm afraid.* And the man's answer... *No, you're right.* Rose's dancing eyes turned suddenly serious. "Oh sorry, Poppy, I'm going on and on about me and I never once asked about you. I'll shut up and do nothing but listen from now on." She pretended to zip up her mouth, then spoke out of the tiniest crack so I could only just make out what she was saying. "You have my undivided attention. Please continue."

I couldn't help laughing, because Rose was practically going cross-eyed she was staring at me so hard.

"There's nothing much to tell really..." It was funny but I suddenly didn't want Rose to know what the lady had said about me not being flexible enough. "They looked at Tamsyn a lot...*and* Jasmine...and the lady wrote stuff in her notepad...and Sophie said they asked Miss Coralie if they could come back another time."

"Did they look at *you*, Poppy?"

"Well...not really..." But Rose's eyes were so

sympathetic that in the end I *did* tell her. "I heard the woman say to the man that I wasn't flexible enough."

"Are you sure she was saying that? I mean, how could she tell? Were you all doing the splits or something?"

"No...but I definitely heard her saying it. I guess they just know... And anyway, Tamsyn was showing off stretching her legs on the *barre* even though we'd been in the centre for ages."

"Wow! You were doing *centre* work! They only stayed for the *barre* in our class. Then off they went – and not very quietly either – well, the man tried to tiptoe but the woman was clicking away on her high heels. I thought Miss Coralie would blow a fuse, but she just kept teaching away as though people clicked in and out of her class every day of the year!"

Rose is in the other Year Six class, and while her class was doing games in the afternoon we had art. I kept thinking about our conversation and wondering about who those visitors could have been and why they'd stayed for such a short time in Rose's class, but watched our class for ages, *and* asked to come back again. Did that mean they'd made a decision about Rose's class already, but they weren't sure about ours?

We had to paint the scenery for the play that Year Three are going to do. My friend Mia and I were painting one of the panels for the back of the stage. It was already standing up against the back wall. The trouble was I was so deep in thought wondering who the visitors were that I kept going over the same bit until it looked far too dark compared to Mia's and everyone else's painting.

"Poppy! Are you trying to make a hole in the cardboard? You're spending far too long on the same part. What *are* you thinking about?"

I couldn't tell Mrs. Townsend what I was thinking about, but at least I didn't go red. I just said sorry and moved on to another part of the scenery, but inside my head I was getting more and more excited because the thought had turned into an important decision. I *would* exercise hard all week because the visitors were coming back. If I worked and worked from the very moment I got home from school until I went to bed, I might be able to do the sideways splits by the next lesson, *and* put my whole top half flat on the floor. And then I might get picked. Yes!!!

At the end of art Mrs. Townsend said she wanted a quick word before we went back to the classroom. "I want you all to remember to take your maths books home and finish the page we were on, then do the next one. Remember what I told you about the importance of doing the homework you're set and handing it in promptly. This is what you'll have to do every day at secondary school, so let's get into good habits now."

"When do we have to hand it in, Miss?" asked one of the boys.

"Tomorrow, of course, Jim."

A groan went round the class, but it wasn't half as bad as the groan that went round my body. On this day of all days I didn't want to spend time doing homework. And maths always takes me ages. The fastest way to get it done, would be to whizz through and do all the easy questions, then phone Jasmine. She'd easily be able to work out the answers to the rest.

As I was going out of the hall I caught sight of my reflection in the big mirror on the end wall. Then Rose suddenly appeared in the reflection. She was standing in the hall doorway and I thought how much more of a dancer than me she looked. She's so slim and little – petite, Mum calls her – even though she's the tough tomboy type and probably the strongest girl in Year Six because of all the gym she's done. It was no wonder those talent scouts kept looking at her.

Never mind, I told myself as I walked along the corridor back to the classroom, it's flexibility they're looking for, not petiteness, and I'm going to work so hard that no one will believe it when they see me in class next week. I stretched up another centimetre and pushed the thought of the maths homework to the back of my mind.

3 Just for one Week

Mum picked me and my little brother Stevie up from school. The moment we got home I went up to my room, changed into my ballet things and stood in front of the mirror imagining that I was in class with the visitors watching. I stood in fifth position and pulled up out of my ribs. But no matter how much I pulled up I didn't look like Rose. I felt a flurry in my stomach. (That's my name for a flutter of worry.)

Don't be silly, Poppy! It's not how thin you are, it's how flexible you are.

I decided to warm up to my favourite piece of

music which is *Waltz of the Flowers* from *The Nutcracker Suite.* My chest of drawers is my *barre* because it's exactly the right height and when I turn sideways I can see myself in the mirror. Really, I was dying to start stretching my legs and my back hard, but I know from Miss Coralie how important it is to get thoroughly warmed up before you start stretching, otherwise you could strain something.

Next I put on my CD of *Coppélia* and started my leg stretches at the *barre* – well, at the chest of drawers. My right leg has always been a bit more supple than my left one. In fact my right side is altogether stronger than my left. All the same I wanted my whole body to be more flexible so I was going to work both sides equally. I spent ages doing stretches, balancing on one leg and holding the other foot up high, trying to press my leg against my body. But I couldn't straighten the knee completely. I just wasn't supple enough.

After that I sat on the floor with my legs as wide apart as I could make them go, which wasn't anywhere near the sideways splits. Then I laid my top half over my right leg and waited until the hamstring muscle at the back of my thigh had relaxed into the stretch before I tried to go down a bit further. It was tempting to force myself to go straight down as hard as I could, but I knew it worked much better if you did it very slowly and gradually. The second time my hamstring relaxed I really felt as though I was making a difference, so I did it again and again until there was no more stretch left and if my hamstring had been a rubber band it would have snapped. My leg was hurting like mad but I didn't care. This was important. Very important.

"Poppy! Tea's ready!"

Oh no! I wasn't balanced yet. I had to do the other leg. Usually when Mum calls out that tea is ready it means that she wants me to go downstairs right away and help lay the table, but I couldn't do that today. I started doing the same thing that I'd done on the right side and immediately felt how much stiffer my left side was.

"Poppy, did you hear me?"

She wasn't cross yet. I had a bit more time, but all the same I'd have to speed up. I put my hands round my ankle, stretched my knee and began to gently pull. Immediately I felt a sudden jab of pain near the top of my leg. So then I told myself off for going too quickly, and gave my leg a waggle around to ease it up again.

"Poppy, can you come down, please?"

But I couldn't. My left leg hadn't had half as much flexing as my right. "Won't be a sec, Mum. I'm just finishing...my...homework."

"Come now, please. It's getting cold. And bring your homework down so I can see."

Uh-oh. Maybe that wasn't such a great

excuse after all. I sighed a big sigh as I pulled on my jeans and top.

Stevie was racing round the table balancing an egg on a spoon when I went into the kitchen. "Bet you can't do this, Poppy!"

"Why can't *you* set the table, Stevie? Why is it always me?"

"'Cos you're a girl and you're older." He didn't stop.

Mum heard him though and grabbed the egg off the spoon as he went past the next time. "We'll have none of that sexual discrimination in this house, young man! You can get the knives and forks out."

"What's secshall scrimintion? You can't tell me off for doing something I've never even heard of."

"It means that just because you're a boy it doesn't stop you helping round the house. Now get on with it!" Mum turned back to the cooker.

I gave Stevie a cross look, but actually I was

feeling quite pleased with him because he'd made Mum forget all about my homework.

"I'm not really all that hungry," I told Mum when she was dishing out the sausages. "I'll just have one."

Really I was thinking that the sooner I finished eating, the faster I could get back to my practice.

Stevie's eyes lit up. "Can I have Poppy's, Mum?"

"Well, let's see how you get on with your own first." Then she turned back to me. "Did you have a big lunch?"

"Er...yes... Huge."

She smiled. "That's fine then."

If there were eating competitions for seven year olds, Stevie would win every time. I've never seen anyone eat so fast and so much.

Mum must have been thinking the same as me. "I don't know where you put it, Stevie!"

"Can I have some more juice?"

She nodded and I watched him as he slithered

out of his seat and half walked, half slid on his socks to the fridge.

"Where *does* he put it, Mum?" It sounded like a bit of a stupid question, but it just slipped out before I'd really thought about it.

"He's a growing boy using up a lot of energy."

"But I'm a growing girl and I'm not as skinny as Stevie."

"Well, everyone's body works differently, doesn't it?"

Mum had gone to make herself another cup of tea and I could tell she wasn't really interested in the conversation. But *I* was, because a picture of Rose's reflection in the school-hall mirror had just flashed through my mind.

"Do you think Rose is much thinner than me, Mum?"

She was spooning out the tea bag. I saw her stop right in the middle of putting it in the bin. "She's just a thin sort of person, isn't she? We're all made differently."

"So...she's much thinner than me?"

"Course she is," said Stevie.

"She's just got a smaller frame...and don't speak with your mouth full, Stevie." Mum came back to the table and stirred her tea for ages in a sort of daydream, even though she doesn't even take sugar.

"Your clanky spoon's making my head hurt," Stevie interrupted her.

"Sorry," said Mum, stopping quickly. She looked at me and then I realized what she'd been daydreaming about. "I hope you're not eating less because you think it'll make you as thin as Rose."

"No, I told you, I had a big lunch, that's all."

"Good, because you're perfect as you are. And you need food for energy and strength." She was giving me one of her heavy looks, where her eyes are speaking to me as well as her mouth.

"Can I get down now?"

She nodded and I rushed out quickly so she wouldn't suddenly remember the homework.

Up in my room, I sat down on the floor, hugged my knees and thought how unfair it is that Rose has got flexibility and thinness, Jasmine has got technique and brain, and what have I got? Miss Coralie says that my expression is my strength, but that doesn't count, does it? Anyone can have expression. You just have to remember to dance with the top half of your body as well as the bottom half.

I peeled off my jeans and top and remembered Mum's words. *You're perfect as you are.* But I'm not, am I? Rose is perfect. Maybe those visitors wouldn't have minded so much about how flexible I was if I'd been lovely and thin like Rose.

People go on diets to get thin, don't they? Jasmine's mum once lost loads of weight before she went on holiday because she wanted to look good in her bikini on the beach. I could find out from Jasmine how she did it and whether it would work in only a week.

I jumped up with excitement about my new plan and was about to go and phone Jasmine when I changed my mind. Jasmine would say it was wrong to try and lose weight. Her dad's a doctor and he's got very strict ideas about health. He doesn't think ballet's good for you in the first place and, of course, Jasmine doesn't agree about that. I'm certain that her dad would think it's bad for people our age to go on diets, though, and unfortunately, I've got the feeling Jasmine would probably agree with him.

But surely it wouldn't be bad for you if you only did it for one week. I could just pretend to Mum that I'd had a big lunch every day at school, and then eat hardly any tea. That would make me much thinner by next Tuesday. Then once I'd got the visitors actually *looking* at the new thin me, they'd soon see how much more flexible I was. I could just imagine them whispering to each other in a lovely puff of amazement... *We must have got it wrong last week. This child is actually one of the most supple in the class!*

A little cloud was trying to scud its way across my lovely sunny thoughts, but I just ignored it.

Come on, Poppy! Get to work! You've got one week. Let's see if you can do it!

4 Quick Thinking

It wasn't till I was going into my classroom the next morning that I realized I'd completely forgotten about the homework. Mia came rushing up to ask me what answer I had for number fourteen.

I clapped my hand over my mouth. "I've not done it!"

"Well, I made it seventy-six..."

"No, I mean I haven't done any of it. Can I copy yours?" I did praying hands and my most pleading eyes. "Pleeeeeease?"

She handed me her book, but I'd hardly

started copying when Mrs. Townsend came in and smiled round the class. "Good morning, everybody. Can I have your maths books on my desk, please?"

Mia gave me a worried look and my heart started popping as I handed back her maths book. I didn't want to have to make up an excuse in front of the whole class because they'd all stare at me, so I just shrank at my desk and hoped Mrs. Townsend wouldn't notice that one book was missing. I could go and see her in the staff room at morning break. That'd give me time to make up a really good reason why I hadn't done it.

"Poppy, I didn't see you bring yours up?"

I gulped and felt my cheeks warming up. "I...I...forgot about it... Sorry."

"That's not like you, Poppy." She didn't seem cross, though, just rather serious. "Make sure you remember to do it tonight."

*

As the day went on my legs started to hurt. I knew why. It was because I'd overstretched my muscles the night before. I must have done about three hours' stretching altogether. Standing in the dinner queue with Rose I started getting anxious in case I was too stiff for practising later. If only I could get to work right there and then in the queue. It was such a waste of time just standing around, especially as I didn't even want any dinner. Well, I *did* but…

For breakfast I'd had a big bowl of cornflakes, only I'd tipped most of them in the bin when Mum hadn't been looking. At break we're allowed a snack and Mum always lets me help myself to a cereal bar from the cupboard, or a piece of fruit, but I didn't take anything today and just pretended to Rose that I'd forgotten it. She kept offering me bites of her apple but I said I was full up with breakfast. So now I was starving but I was still determined to eat as little as possible.

The further up the queue we moved, the more I could smell my favourite school dinner – chicken and mushroom pie with rice and peas and carrots. I could have easily eaten two big pieces and loads of rice and vegetables, and I very nearly changed my mind about getting thin for the next ballet lesson. But then I made myself get a picture in my head of the two visitors smiling and announcing to everyone that Poppy Vernon was the chosen one.

When we were practically at the front of the queue, I wrinkled up my nose, like I'd planned to and whispered to Rose, "Yuk, that looks horrible. It's not normally as runny as that."

"I can't see any difference," said Rose, sticking out her plate and holding it there for ages so the dinner lady would pile on more.

"I don't know where you put it, a little squirt like you!"

If someone had said that to me, I would have been the happiest girl in the world.

Rose went off to sit down and then it was my turn. I gulped. "Only a small slice please, and just a bit of rice, thanks."

"You won't get fat on that, dear!" joked the serving lady loudly.

"I'm not all that hungry..."

But she was serving the next person so I rushed off to find Rose. And as I sat down, I told her I was going to ask if I could stay in and do my homework after lunch. I knew she wasn't going to be very pleased, but I had to get the homework done in school time, so I could concentrate on nothing but stretches once I got home.

"Can't you do it tonight? I'll be bored on my own."

At least she hadn't noticed how little there was on my plate. Now all I had to do was to tell her a little fib about all the stuff Mum had been collecting over the last week, for a jumble sale.

"I won't have time after school. Mum says

I've got to help her sort everything out into bags for that jumble sale." I pulled a face to show I wasn't impressed. But inside I felt horrible for lying to Rose.

I ate slowly to make my food last longer. And as Rose always eats quickly, we finished at the same time.

She was already jumping up. "You take the dirties and I'll go up for pudding. Chocolate sponge roll. Brill! I'll get us big pieces, you watch!"

"Actually I don't think I've got time. I have to go and find Mrs. Townsend."

So while Rose was eating her pudding I went to ask Mrs. Townsend if I could stay in to do the maths.

"Save your homework for *home* time, Poppy. I'd much rather you were out in the fresh air."

I nodded, but inside my head the homework was starting to turn into a big worry. Crashing about. Getting in the way of my practice.

5 Hurting

We always say "I'm starving" when we feel hungry and "I'm hungry" when we feel a bit peckish, but until now I didn't know what either of those two words really meant. I still don't know what starving means, but I've realized about hunger, and it hurts.

I was lying on my back on my bedroom floor, raising and lowering my legs one at a time. *They* were hurting too, because the muscles were even stiffer than they had been at lunchtime. I put my hands round my waist to see if all the not-eating was working, and I definitely felt thinner.

I squeezed my waist until it was as thin as it would go and felt as though I was pushing little zings of happiness right up to my throat. This was how thin I could be by next Tuesday – even when I was standing up normally and not pulling in at all.

Five days to go. That thought made the zings spread out into fizzy flashes of nervousness. I had to make myself as flexible as Tamsyn and as thin as Rose in only five days. I'd better stop wasting time and get on with it. It felt like such an effort, though. I just didn't seem to have any strength. Maybe I should do some backbends to give my legs a chance to recover. I rolled over onto my stomach and stretched my neck and the top of my back as far as they would go. Then I pushed on my hands to make the bottom of my back bend more, and at the same time I curled my legs and pointed my toes hard until my whole body was shaking with the effort. But still I couldn't quite make my toes touch my head. I wanted to see how near they were to touching, so I took my mirror off the wall and propped it up against the bed, then went in to the backbend again.

Pooh! It looked as though there were still about ten centimetres to go. I'd thought I was much closer than that. I flopped down sadly and wished that Mum would hurry up and say that tea was ready. It wouldn't matter about eating quite a lot now, would it? After all, I'd done very well during the rest of the day.

The doorbell rang when I was in my third backbend. *It must be someone collecting for something,* I thought. But next minute my bedroom door opened and there stood Jasmine with a great big smile on her face.

"Hi, Jasmine! What are *you* doing here?"

"Papa's away!" Jasmine's Mum is French so Jasmine always calls her dad Papa and her mum Maman. She was gabbling away excitedly. "Maman said I had to come to aerobics with her because she didn't want to leave me at home on my own. I've been before and it's really boring sitting in the corner, reading. But we had to drop off some jumble for your mum, and now your mum's invited me to tea! Isn't it good?"

I felt guilty then because I knew I should have been on top of the world to see Jasmine during the week. Apart from ballet on Tuesdays, I don't usually see her because she has so much homework from her school and then she has a tutor one day and her piano lesson another. Plus, her dad is very strict and usually only lets her have people round or go to people's houses at the weekend.

She suddenly shut my bedroom door, grabbed my hand and said, "Guess what?"

"What?"

"You know those visitors?"

My heart started to beat faster. "Yes."

"Well, Eleanor Little from my class at school goes to the Homeleigh Ballet School and she said there were two people watching the class, and when she described them I just knew they were the same people who came to *our* class."

"And who are they?" I asked in a squeak.

Jasmine's eyes widened. "They're looking for someone to do a proper ballet dance in the pantomime at the Carlington Bay Theatre. *And* they're looking in about twenty-five different ballet schools altogether! So isn't it good that they're actually coming back to Miss Coralie's to have another look?"

My heart was thumping like mad. I was desperate to go back to my practice. It seemed more important than ever now, even though a little voice was telling me that if they were coming back, it definitely wasn't because of *me*.

"That's amazing!" I managed to say. "D-did Eleanor tell you anything else about it?"

Jasmine shook her head. "Except that it's definitely only one person they want."

"Well, shall we do some practice then?" I

said, trying not to sound as though it was the most urgent thing in the world.

Jasmine's eyes twinkled. "I've got another surprise." She pulled a video out of her bag and held it out with a flourish. "Look! *The Nutcracker!* It was on Sky last night. It's the Kirov Ballet. We could watch it right now!"

I didn't know what to say. How could I tell Jasmine that I really wanted to practise instead of watching *The Nutcracker,* when she knows that it's my favourite ballet and it was obvious I'd already been practising?

"I don't mind if you want to keep it and watch it yourself first, Jasmine..." I said carefully. "It'd be a bit of a waste of our time together if we're just watching a video. Why don't we do some ballet?"

"But I didn't bring my things."

"You could borrow my pink leotard..."

"The one that you wore last year? That'd never fit me."

"Well, what about just staying like you are..." I knew that was a terrible idea even as I was saying it because of course Jasmine couldn't do ballet in her school uniform. "Or, *I* know, you could wear my jogging bottoms and one of my tops."

She was looking really puzzled now and it was no wonder really. I must have sounded a bit mad going on and on like that.

"Why don't we just watch the video?" she said quietly.

"Tea's ready!" called Mum in a sing-song happy voice. She loves it that Jasmine is one of my two best friends. She says she's a good influence on me.

We sat round the tea table and I could hardly wait to start eating I was so hungry. I kept on trying to make the picture of the two visitors come into my head, but it wasn't working. The only pictures inside my head were of food. My first few mouthfuls didn't even seem to touch the sides they went down so fast. And I couldn't join in the conversation because I would have had to slow down.

"Someone's enjoying the spag bol!" said Mum. Then she carried on chatting to Jasmine. I wasn't joining in at all, but I did hear Jasmine say something about how she'd been planning to read a book during the aerobics class because she'd done her homework. The moment I heard the word *homework*, I started worrying that Mum might remember about *my* homework, but she didn't say anything about it, thank goodness. Then I had an idea. If Jasmine helped me, I'd get it done much quicker than I'd ever be able to on my own.

As soon as we'd finished tea and gone back up to my room I asked her if she could look at it. We sat on my bed together and she seemed to be taking ages just staring at it with a frown on her face.

"Are you supposed to show the workings?"

I nodded.

"Have you got a ruler?"

I whipped one out of my bag even though I just wanted to get it done. I didn't really care about it being all neat and everything.

Jasmine looked round my room. I knew she was wondering what we could rest on, because I haven't got a desk like she has. "Shall we go down to the table?"

"We can't Jazz, because Mum thinks I've already done the homework, you see...last night..." I giggled a bit nervously and then wondered why I felt nervous. After all, it was only Jasmine.

"Oh...well what should I rest on?"

I gave her my encyclopedia and waited for her to start. Why was it taking so long? My whole body was dying to get back to stretching – well, nearly my whole body. My stomach was uncomfortable because of all the spaghetti bolognese I'd eaten. Why had I been so stupid and greedy? I never normally ate that much. I'd completely spoiled my good day now.

"Whoops!" Jasmine had knocked the mirror over with her foot. "Sorry. What's it doing down here?"

"I...I was...checking my feet in the *battements frappés.*" The truth seemed more private than ever now. In fact it had turned into an actual secret – even from my best friends. How could I tell them I was so desperate to be noticed by the talent spotters that I was trying to be the thinnest, most flexible person in the class in just one week? But it would be worth it, to get to dance on a real stage in a proper pantomime.

"I understand the first question," I said to Jasmine, to try to get her to hurry up with the maths. I grabbed the book off her and started scribbling. "Is this right?"

"Yes, but haven't you got to write it neatly?"

That gave me a brain wave. "You'll be much

quicker and neater than me, Jasmine. Do you want to do it for me, while I keep practising?"

The moment I'd said it I felt horrible and mean. Poor Jasmine had come round to watch a video with me and I was making her do my homework.

She sounded a bit worried. "Won't the teacher see that it's not your usual writing?"

I hadn't thought of that. "If you do them in rough, I'll copy them into my book later." I gave her my notepad and went over to my chest of drawers.

"There. I've done the second one. D'you want me to explain?"

"That's okay, I'll copy them later," I said, going straight into *développés*.

Jasmine looked at her watch. "I don't think Mum'll be much longer now. What about if I just do the ones you don't understand and then we'll have time for a bit of the video?"

I felt really selfish but I couldn't help it. I *had*

to stretch. It was the most important thing in my life. Jasmine's face looked so puzzled and sad though. Maybe I ought to leave it till after she'd gone. Yes, I'd be able to concentrate better then. And I could carry on as late as I wanted, even after bedtime. *Even* after Mum and Dad had gone to bed.

I sat on the bed beside Jasmine and made another plan. Not only would I work until at least midnight, I would also pay myself back for spoiling my good food day. The next day I would have no breakfast, hardly any lunch and hardly any tea. Yes!

Perfect plan, Poppy.

6 Confusion and Panic

It's half past midnight and I can't get to sleep. My brain won't switch off and neither will my body. Even though I'm lying in bed, my toes are still stretching and my legs are turned out. When I put my hands round my waist it feels as though it's gone back to normal and I can't wait for the end of tomorrow because I'll be thin again by then.

I've set my alarm for six-thirty so I can finish off the maths questions because Jasmine and I only did the first four in the end. After Mum and Dad had said night to me, I got out of bed and did more stretches in my pyjamas. I knew I'd have to be really careful about the noise, and listen like mad for footsteps on the stairs. When I heard them coming up to bed I quickly got under my duvet, waited till their bedroom door closed then got up again and carried on.

I should be absolutely exhausted by now, but I feel as though I'm running down the longest corridor in the world, chasing sleep and trying to make it stop and turn round and creep inside my brain to switch it off.

Come on, sleep... Come on...

"Come on, Poppy!"

"What? Who's that?"

I shot awake and sat bolt upright, my eyes wide open. Mum was standing there. "Hurry up! You're going to be late! I woke you up ages ago. You must have fallen back to sleep."

I got out of bed and stood there, all confused. What had happened to my alarm? Why hadn't it gone off? I snatched it up, and saw right away that I'd set it for p.m. instead of a.m. Then everything came flooding back and I went into a big panic. The maths! I was supposed to be getting up early to do it. I *had* to hand it in today. I couldn't make up any more excuses.

Mum rushed off downstairs calling back to me to get ready as quickly as possible, then come down for breakfast. My heart flipped over and over as I stumbled into the bathroom. In no time I was washed, dressed, with my hair brushed and pulled back into a ponytail.

Right, Poppy. Calm down.

I pulled out my maths book and wrote out question number five, then started to try and do it the way Jasmine had shown me with the other four. It had seemed so easy last night but this morning I couldn't remember a single thing she'd said.

Stevie was racing upstairs. "Mum says hurry up and come down to breakfast."

"Tell her, it's okay. I'll help myself to something."

He clattered away and I tried again with number five, but I knew I'd never be able to do it, and even if I *could* there were still ten more after that. Maybe if we got to school early enough and I went straight into the classroom instead of chatting to Rose, I'd have time to copy off Mia. But then I remembered that Mia had handed her book in with all the others so I couldn't even do that. It was hopeless. Mrs. Townsend was going to be so mad with me. I flopped down on my bed.

Think, Poppy. Think.

"Are you all right, Pops?"

That was Dad. He was peering round my bedroom door looking all worried. Which is what gave me my brilliant idea. At least, it flashed into my head as just a single idea, but in no time at all it had grown three more. If I said I *wasn't* all right, I wouldn't have to go to school.

That would mean I wouldn't have to hand in my homework, I'd have loads of time for stretching and, best of all, you don't have to eat anything at all when you're ill, especially if it's a stomach bug.

I was so pleased with myself that it was quite difficult keeping my eyes droopy and my voice groany. "I feel a bit sick, Dad."

His face turned into a big creased-up frown. "Hang on... I'll...fetch Mum."

When he'd gone I closed my eyes. It's easier to tell lies if you don't have to look at the person. Then Mum came in and felt my head. She bobbed down beside me so our faces were on exactly the same level. I could feel my eyelids fluttering because they didn't really feel like being closed.

"Has this sick feeling only just come on, Poppy?" Her voice sounded a bit suspicious.

I nodded.

"Does your stomach hurt?"

I shook my head. "I just feel sick...and tired."

"Well, I'm sorry love, but I can't get someone to come and sit with you at this late hour. I think you'll be fine to go to school. You've certainly got plenty of colour. There's no way I can ask Karen to cover for me at work. It's just not fair."

Mum works as a receptionist at a hotel called The Cramer. She hasn't been doing the job very long and she just does Wednesdays and Fridays. Karen does Mondays, Tuesdays and Thursdays.

"Can't you just ask Karen if she'll swap? I feel terrible!"

"No, not at such short notice."

"Could Dad have a day off?"

"No, that's out of the question." Mum frowned even more. Then she went all brisk. "Come on, you don't look ill, Poppy. Have you got everything you need for school?"

She was looking round my room and any second now she'd see my maths homework book. I jumped up and scooped it into my bag.

"There you are, see! You're getting back to your usual lively self already!" She threw me a *got-you* look as she rushed out.

Now what was I going to do?

I went into the classroom with a hammering heart. I was about to tell another lie and I was dreading it. After Mum had gone out of my room, I'd taken my maths book straight out of my school bag and hidden it under the bed so I could pretend I'd done all the homework, but just forgotten to bring the book to school.

"Morning, everybody."

Mrs. Townsend was standing at the front and I hadn't even realized she'd come in. Inside my chest something squeezed.

"Places, please. Register."

I don't like it when she misses out words when she's talking. It means she's in a no-nonsense mood. I went to my place and tried to look completely normal.

"Poppy...homework. All done?"

This was it. I had to make myself smile and nod as I opened my bag. Then I had to pretend to search and search and look puzzled, then alarmed. When I looked up, her eyes were on me. Not moving.

"Sorry, Mrs. Townsend. I must have left it at home."

Still her eyes didn't move and I couldn't help the redness that was flooding into my cheeks.

"Never mind, Poppy. I'll see it on Monday."

A moment later she was taking the register and everyone was answering to their names. "Yes, Mrs. Townsend. Yes, Mrs. Townsend." Just like we do every day. It felt funny today, though, because I knew I'd made her cross, and yet instead of speaking angry words to me she was just breathing out crossness so it hung around in the air.

7 Spilling Secrets

That afternoon I fell asleep in the classroom. Mrs. Townsend was talking about different types of bridges. I just remember thinking what a nice word *cantilever* was and then the next thing I knew Mia was nudging me and whispering my name. When I opened my eyes I got a shock to see that I was at school and at first I thought it might still be part of my dream.

"Aren't you feeling well, Poppy?" asked Mrs. Townsend, coming over to my desk. "Or are you just tired?"

I said I wasn't well and she asked me if Mum

was picking me up at the end of school, but I said it was Rose's mum.

It's been brilliant going home with Rose on Fridays since Mum started her job. Rose's mum does baking for the freezer on Friday afternoons and the kitchen always smells of cooking and warmth. Rose and I usually choreograph a dance together and make up Jasmine's part, too, so that the next day we can all dance it together.

When we got to Rose's I managed to say no to a piece of snowy lemon cake, then Rose and I went upstairs and I talked loudly every time my stomach rumbled. If I'd been at my own house I think I would have gone straight down to the kitchen and eaten anything I could find, I was so hungry by then. I'd only had a teeny bit of school dinner, so it was no wonder really.

Rose usually lets me do most of the choreography for the dance, then Jasmine helps the next day, because she's the best at arranging steps. I deliberately choreographed a lovely big *développé* into my part, where I had to slowly uncurl my leg to the side as high as it would go. Rose had got a classical CD of the ballet *Sylvia* from the library. We both love the bit in the music where the horns play a hunting tune.

"Let's pretend we're famous dancers and everyone is watching us!" said Rose with sparkling eyes staring straight ahead. I think she was imagining an audience at that moment. Then she turned to me and grabbed my hand. "Hey, that might *really* happen to someone at Miss Coralie's, mightn't it!"

I didn't want to talk about it because being picked to dance in the pantomime was part of the private world inside my head, but Rose sounded really excited.

"We'll find out on Tuesday, won't we?" She grabbed my other hand and started skipping me round in crazy circles. I felt suddenly clumsy and stupid doing that because I'm not a mad person like Rose. I'm too self-conscious.

We put the music back on and Rose turned back into her serious ballet self, while I went off imagining those talent spotters watching me and whispering to each other...

My goodness, what a change! This girl will be ideal, don't you think?

Absolutely perfect, yes!

When it came to my *développé* bit, I don't know what happened. Maybe it was because of my imagination making me dance better, or the music, but I did the best one I'd ever done. My leg was definitely stretching higher than usual.

"Hey, that looks so brilliant, Poppy!" said Rose, standing still.

I pointed my toe harder than ever and felt as though an army of helium balloons was lifting me up up up to the ceiling because Rose was watching me with her head on one side. "I wish I could do it like that, Poppy."

It was such a dreamy moment. I'd worked and worked and now Rose thought I was even more flexible than her. It was unbelievable.

"Shall we put the music back to the beginning and start again?" I said, wanting to feel that lovely feeling all over again.

"Yeah, in a sec. Just let me have a go at that *devil pay* thing."

And when she did it, it was as though the helium balloons had suddenly grown old and withered and were slowly falling to the ground, because Rose's leg went miles higher than mine. It pointed upwards, not sideways. And she looked so professional with her tight muscles and strong body.

"Right, show me what to do with my head, Poppy. And my arms."

I could hardly keep the sadness out of my voice. "It doesn't matter about your head and your arms. It's your legs that count."

She laughed. "Don't be silly, it's your whole body! That's what you're so good at. Come on! Show me how to make it look like yours."

I said I didn't really know how to and she made a face as though she was seriously disappointed. But how *could* she have been when her leg had gone so much higher than mine?

We did the dance twice more but it wasn't the same. I was too fed up to do it properly. When Mum came to pick me up, Rose's mum wrapped up a big piece of snowy lemon cake in tinfoil for me to take home. I was going to put it in the bin in my room, but I made the mistake of having a little peep at it first, and it smelled so good that I ate the whole lot before I'd even realized.

I sat down on the floor to try and get myself in the mood to do more stretching but I was too cross with myself for eating the lemon cake.

Never mind, it's only one little piece of cake, I kept telling myself. But it was no good.

For tea it was beefburgers in soft white rolls. I tried so hard to nibble slowly, but I took bigger and bigger mouthfuls and when the beefburger had disappeared I gobbled two bowls of strawberry ice cream with wafer biscuits. Then I curled up tight on the settee and watched television until bedtime.

The next day, Jasmine and Rose both came to my house in the afternoon. Jasmine arrived first and wanted me to show her the dance that Rose and I had worked out.

"Shall we just wait till Rose gets here?" I said. "It works better with the music."

The real reason I didn't want to show her was because I was still too gloomy. All the sadness that had clung round me last night wouldn't go away. Even when Rose turned up, and Stevie insisted on having a boxing match with her, which made Jasmine giggle so much she fell off the settee, I still couldn't find the smallest bubble of laughter inside me.

"What's the matter, Poppy?" Jasmine asked me later when we were up in my room again.

I shrugged and said I didn't really know.

"I bet I know how to make you happy," said Rose, putting on the CD of *Sylvia*. I sat on the bed while Rose showed Jasmine what we'd made up.

"And this is the bit where Poppy does her *devil pay,"* said Rose with a proud note in her voice.

"*Développé*!" Jasmine corrected her.

I wished Rose hadn't mentioned that. "Show Jazz, Poppy." She turned to Jasmine. "It's so brilliant the way she does it, you know!"

"It's not," I said, trying not to sound too grumpy. "Rose can do it much better."

"Let's see," said Jasmine.

So I showed her, even though I absolutely did *not* want to.

"You're not doing it how you did it yesterday," said Rose, putting her hands on her waist and pretending to be cross.

"I just don't feel like it today," I said. And then I felt really stupid because I knew that tears were starting to come into my eyes and I didn't think I could stop them.

"Oh Poppy, what's the matter?" said Jasmine.

And Rose wrapped her arms tight round me, which is what she always does if she thinks either of us is unhappy.

"I don't know," I said through a gulp.

"You *must* know," said Rose, breaking off her hug to look me in the eyes. "Here, you need a bit of solidarity!" Then she pressed her thumb against mine and her other thumb against Jasmine's, so Jasmine and I joined thumbs too. It's a thing that the three of us do for luck, or just for friendship really. We call it a thumb-thumb.

I tried to find the words that might explain how I felt, but my feelings were impossible to put into words because they were too tied up with my secret longing to be picked. All I knew was that when Jasmine and Rose had gone home I'd have to start stretching again and I wouldn't let myself stop for hours and hours and hours because I couldn't allow this big, big chance to slip away. But it was all so hard. And it hurt. It hurt my legs, it hurt my stomach, it hurt my brain. But worst of all it hurt inside. Yes, that was definitely the worst bit.

8 The Stars in the Sky

"This is a very important day!" I said to the stars outside my window on Sunday evening. There were masses and masses of them all over the sky and even that seemed to be important. I decided that they were all famous people who'd died but their memory was living on. Then I chose two of the stars to be famous dancers. They were both small, but very very bright and one of them I named Margot Fonteyn and the other Anna Pavlova. When I turned away from the window it looked as though my bedroom walls were covered in glitter because my eyes hadn't adjusted to the light.

"I did it!" I said to my reflection in the mirror. Then I turned sideways so I could admire my thinness. This was the first day that I'd managed to go for a whole day without eating proper meals, in fact without eating much at all, and I thought I could see the difference. All the other days had been fine until teatime and then I'd spoiled everything by stuffing myself full as a cushion, just because of being hungry. I'd never been strong-willed enough until today. But now it was nearly bedtime and I'd actually done it.

If Mum hadn't had to take Stevie to an away match, I wouldn't have been able to eat so little. But Dad was in charge at lunchtime and he didn't even notice that I tipped most of my chicken and chips into the bin. In the afternoon I went round to Rose's, but I came back in time for tea. Then Dad went out as soon as Mum came home, so I just told Mum that I was still full up from lunchtime. Easy!

It was a bit early but I decided to go to bed anyway, then I wouldn't be tempted to go downstairs and raid the food cupboards and the fridge. Just the thought of that lovely quiche that Stevie and Mum had eaten and the rest of that velvety chocolate mousse made my mouth fill up with saliva, so I quickly rushed to the bathroom to clean my teeth. Standing in front of the bathroom mirror I felt a bit dizzy and thought my face looked rather pale, but I didn't mind because my freckles looked better on a pale background. Then my stomach did a massive rumble and I wondered whether there might be an apple in the kitchen. One little apple wouldn't do any harm.

I went out onto the landing and got that dizzy feeling again, only this time I felt sick too. I'd better tell Mum. So I set off downstairs, but had to clutch the banister because there seemed to be something wrong with my legs. And my face felt awful, as though all the blood was draining out of it.

"Mum!" I called out from the bottom step.

Then I fell down on the floor with a crash.

I don't remember much about what happened right after I'd fainted, except for Mum telling me to put my head between my legs. She spoke to me gently and soothingly at first, but then I heard her and Dad whispering in worried voices. I hoped they weren't saying anything about me not eating enough, but I had the horrible feeling they might be, because when one of the Year Six girls fainted in assembly once, the first question the teacher asked was whether she'd been eating properly.

Dad got me a glass of water and helped me upstairs, then went back down. But Mum stayed in my room. I was lying on my bed and she was staring out of my window at the stars, just like I'd been doing earlier. She stayed there for ages and when I looked round, I saw her worried frown.

"Isn't it a beautiful, starry night?" I said, to try and stop her thinking too much.

"You're right, it *is* beautiful, Poppy." Mum closed the curtains, turned round and put both hands on my cheeks for a moment. "Just like you!"

I smiled a bit of a shaky smile. "I think...I'll go to bed now, Mum...to make sure I'm better for school tomorrow."

As soon as I'd spoken, my heart turned over because I remembered that I *still* hadn't done the homework. I was so stupid. If only I'd thought to ask Jasmine to help me with it when we were at Rose's this afternoon.

Mum's next words gave me a massive shock. "Mrs. Townsend phoned me yesterday."

"Mrs. Townsend! My teacher?"

"Yes, I know... She doesn't normally phone parents at the weekend. But she was worried."

I gulped and lay quite still, hoping that there wasn't any pinkness coming into my cheeks.

"I didn't mention it to you because you seemed to have recovered and I thought it must have been one of those twenty-four-hour bugs."

I was slowly realizing why Mrs. Townsend had phoned. Not because of the homework, but because I'd fallen asleep in class. It still seemed a bit scary that she'd actually phoned. I mean, people *do* sometimes fall asleep in the middle of lessons.

"Yes, I think I must have got a bug," I said, trying to sound grown up and sensible. Then I realized that, of course, this was the perfect excuse for fainting. "That must be why I fainted, mustn't it, Mum?"

"Hmm," said Mum and she stared at me for ages. "Still off your food though, aren't you?"

I knew my cheeks were definitely getting red now. "A bit, I suppose," I said, trying to keep my voice normal.

"Mrs. Townsend said you seem to have been off your food all week."

"How does *she* know?" I blurted out without thinking, as I sat up.

"Because she was worried about you and checked with the dinner ladies." Mum's eyes were very grave. They wouldn't let me look away. The words started tumbling out of her mouth faster and faster. "You're not eating at school, Poppy, then you're going mad eating enough for two people when you get home. You're telling lies about your homework and you're falling asleep in class. Today Dad tells me you hardly touched your lunch, and then you pretended to me that you were still full and promptly fainted. I want to know what's going on. And I want the truth!"

It gave me a shock because she'd stopped so suddenly with her lips pursed up tight. I didn't know what to say. She was banging on the door of my private world but I couldn't let her in. I just couldn't. It would spoil my chances of being picked on Tuesday.

"I forgot about my homework, that's all. Only, I knew I'd get into trouble if I told the truth."

"I see." She was waiting for me to carry on and explain about the eating and the sleeping, but those bits weren't so easy to make excuses for, so I stayed quiet.

"And what's all this about not eating? I've told you, you can't make your body look like Rose's by not eating. Nature simply doesn't work like that, and you can't change nature any more than you can change the weather or those stars in the sky."

There was a hard knot of crossness in my throat. Mum didn't know anything, because I *had* made my body thin – maybe not as thin as Rose's, but I'd only done it properly for one day. If I went on doing it and doing it, I'd be like Rose in the end.

"Well nature *does* work like that, actually!" I snapped, then I curled up facing the wall.

"If you carry on not eating, all you'll do is make yourself ill, as you've just proved, and you still won't look like Rose because Rose's body is made differently from yours, just as mine is made differently from...say...Jasmine's mum's. You'd just look like a thinner version of *you.* A thinner, paler, sicklier version. And what would be the point of that?"

"Because it makes you look better when you're dancing if you're thin!" I shouted. "So there!" And I turned onto my tummy and buried my face in the pillow.

There was such a long silence that I began to wonder if Mum had gone out. I wished she *would* go out and leave me alone.

"Is that why you passed grade four? Were you thinner then?"

"No, but..." I said, turning my face just enough to be able to speak.

"And what about the other girls? What about Jasmine?"

"Jasmine doesn't need to be thin because she's so good at dancing in the first place!" I shouted.

"And Tamsyn?"

"She doesn't need to be thin either because she's so flexible."

"And Sophie and Immy and all the others?"

Mum was making me really mad. I started shouting. "They're *all* better than me, okay!"

"Why? Because they're thinner?"

I sat up and yelled right into Mum's face. "No, because they're just better. It's got nothing to do with thinness!"

Then I flopped back and shut my eyes in the horrible silence that was filling up my room.

When Mum spoke next it was in a very gentle voice. "Okay, that's all I wanted to know. Well, nearly all... Just one more question. Have you done your homework?"

I couldn't speak. I'd used up all the words in

my head, and I didn't care about anything any more because that argument had left me with a horrible feeling and I wasn't completely sure why. I shook my head.

Mum went over to the door. "In that case, I suggest you come downstairs, have a nice mug of hot chocolate and let me and Dad help you with it." I heard the door brush against the carpet. "We'll be in the sitting room."

Then she went. And I was left with a hurting throat and tickling cheeks where two tears were sliding down. I wiped my face quickly and lay there in the silence. The trouble was, it wasn't silence. I could still hear the faint little echo of the last words I'd said to Mum.

It's got nothing to do with thinness.

Why had I said that? Whatever in the whole wide world had made me say that? It *was* to do with thinness.

Wasn't it?

I lay there frowning and thinking, until my

brain started hurting with all the confusion. All week long I'd been trying to make myself thin because I thought it was important, and now I'd just told Mum that how good you are at ballet has nothing to do with thinness. And I know it's true. I mean, it's *really* obvious. Anyone knows that. So why have I been trying to be like Rose?

Because she's flexible. Yes, that's the answer. I said the words out loud, so I wouldn't go back to my confused self again. "*Because she's flexible.*" And that has nothing to do with thinness, has it?

Just then my stomach did the biggest rumble in history and I thought about that mug of hot chocolate. Mmm! Yum! I sat up and hugged my knees, my mouth watering. And Mum had said that she and Dad would help me with my homework too. I stayed perfectly still. It was really strange. I felt as though Mum had hammered so hard on the door to my private world, that I'd given in and let my secret thoughts escape. But instead of feeling bad about it, I felt good. I was glad she'd made me see sense.

When I went down, Stevie was sprawled against the beanbag in his pyjamas. He'd been in the bath when I'd fainted so he didn't know anything about it, thank goodness. Mum and Dad were on the settee watching television. There was something different about them, though. I think they were sitting closer together than usual. And the moment they saw me they both jumped up.

Mum gave me an anxious sort of look. "I'll pop it in the microwave. It might have gone a bit cold."

Dad pointed the remote at the telly to switch it off.

"It's cosier in the kitchen. Come on," he said, putting his arm out to me, and smiling. A lump came in my throat. I'd got the best parents in the world. They weren't even cross with me. I was so lucky.

9 Not Flexible Enough

There was great excitement in the changing room on Tuesday. Everyone was talking about the visitors.

"D'you think they'll be here?" said Immy.

"I definitely heard them asking if they could come back," Sophie replied firmly.

"They might have chosen someone from another ballet school," said Isobel. "Someone better than any of us!"

Tamsyn looked up from putting her shoes on. You'd think Isobel had called her a horrible name the way her eyes were flashing. "*This* is the best ballet school round here. Anyone knows that."

"They might be choosing someone from the grade four class right now!" squeaked Lottie.

Jasmine and I exchange a look. I guessed she was thinking about Rose, like I was.

Tamsyn was wearing a cross frown. I knew why. It was because she'd been building up her hopes and didn't want anything to knock them down. *I'd* been like that too, but now I was back to normal, thank goodness. I'd stopped all my silly thoughts about trying to be thin and flexible. Mum and I had talked and talked on Sunday evening after we'd done my homework. She'd explained how seriously bad it was for you to mess about not eating. So I'd tried to explain about the visitors and how it was my dream to be picked and to star in a real theatre production, and how I'd been wishing I was more flexible, but then I'd got all muddled about flexibility and thinness. And Mum had said that if I didn't get chosen this time, it would be sure to happen some other time, and that I should just be myself.

"That's the great thing about dreams, Poppy," she'd said. "You don't ever have to let go of them. Simply save them for the next time!"

"Quick, the other class is coming out," said Sophie, jumping up and bringing me back down to earth.

We all followed her into the corridor and lined up in silence. I watched the faces of the girls coming out and when it got to Rose I raised my eyebrows at her.

"They weren't there," she whispered, shrugging.

It was funny but I wasn't really surprised. In my heart I thought that Isobel was probably right and that they'd already found someone from another ballet school.

"Good afternoon, girls," said Miss Coralie, as we ran in with our usual light steps and found a place on the *barre*.

Our eyes, which are normally focused on a point in front of us, were darting sideways, throwing little questioning glances at Miss Coralie. And in the end, when we'd finished the *barre* work and had been put into our rows for centre work, Tamsyn obviously couldn't bear it any longer.

"Excuse me, Miss Coralie..."

Every muscle in my body tightened. Actually, I think every single muscle in the room tightened.

"Yes, Tamsyn?"

"I was wondering if those two people who watched us last week were coming back today?"

"I believe so, yes." A warm shiver rushed round my body. I was so excited to think I'd be finding out at long last if any one of us had been chosen. Miss Coralie wasn't giving us any more clues, though. She just stood in a perfectly turned-out first position and raised her chin. "*Demi-pliés* and rises in first—"

Not Flexible Enough

"Miss Coralie?"

Lottie had her hand up as though she was at school. I suppose she thought that extra bit of politeness might make up for interrupting when we were about to do an exercise.

Miss Coralie tilted her chin without moving any other part of her body. "Yes, Lottie?"

"Er...sorry...I was just wondering whether you could tell us two teeny things, please?" Lottie carried straight on before Miss Coralie had a chance to reply. "Are they only looking for one person? And what age?"

"As far as I know they're looking for just one girl between the ages of six and twelve, Lottie," Miss Coralie answered in a brisk voice.

"Six!" Tamsyn blurted out. "Would a six year old be good enough?"

"*Good enough* doesn't come into it, Tamsyn," said Miss Coralie in a sharp voice. "It's just a question of rightness. Now, no more talking." Her eyes flashed. "*Demi-pliés*. First position. And..."

The sequence of steps that Miss Coralie made up for us to do was so tricky that only Jasmine could remember it.

"Well done, Jasmine!" said Miss Coralie. "Let's do it a row at a time."

I was in the front row and normally I'd be really nervous because of having to remember something when I haven't had a chance to watch one or two other rows doing it first. But today I was much calmer than usual, because of being used to the idea that I wouldn't be picked. The music seemed to fill the whole room and somehow it seeped right into my body too, and actually made me smile as I danced. It was the most wonderful feeling and I didn't worry at all about making one or two little mistakes. And when I did my *développé* I got a "very nice" from Miss Coralie which gave me a lovely surprise and reminded me of what Rose had said.

Then a big gasp came out of my body. I'd

been so wrapped up in the sequence that I hadn't even realized that the lady who'd visited the class last week was standing at the side. Only she didn't look the same. Instead of her suit and high heels, she was wearing jeans and trainers and a baggy jumper, and her hair was tumbling round her shoulders. And now she was tiptoeing to the front. I saw Tamsyn opening her eyes very wide like a doll and I knew she was getting ready to show off.

When all the rows had had their turn, Miss Coralie told us to get back in our lines for the *révérence*. And afterwards she had a quick word with the lady, then turned back to us.

"I'd like to introduce Miss Tara Knight. I've told her that you're full of questions."

"Thank you, Miss Coralie," said Miss Knight, smiling. "Please call me Tara. Firstly, Denis Rayworth, who was here with me last week, is sorry not to be able to come today. Denis and I are directing the pantomime at the Carlington

Bay Theatre this year. As you know, this is a big event that attracts a good deal of media attention and has packed audiences every night for a month."

I held my breath. We all did.

"The pantomime this year is *Sleeping Beauty*. Now, you may be wondering why we need a ballet dancer for a pantomime. Let me explain. Usually in the Sleeping Beauty story we see the baby Princess's christening party with the good fairies and the bad fairy, and then we don't see the Princess growing up. The story jumps right to her fifteenth birthday. But in *our* version we are going to see what a good singer the Princess is when she's a little girl, and then what a good dancer she is when she's about your age, because these are two of the gifts that the good fairies bestowed upon her. And we're very lucky because we've got Lisa Malloy to do the choreography for the 'dancing princess', as we call her."

Jasmine and I looked at each other. Lisa Malloy was the choreographer of the ballet we'd seen in London for Rose's birthday treat.

"Before we came here last week," Tara went on, "Denis and I came across a girl in another ballet school who we thought would be very suitable for the part, and indeed we nearly settled on her, but then we were so impressed with what we saw at Miss Coralie's that we began to wonder whether it would be possible to have *two* girls playing the same role and doing half the rehearsals each. But we had to forget that idea because the production simply isn't flexible enough."

Tara was still talking, but I wasn't listening any more. Her last words were going round and round in my head, and I was thinking of the whispered conversation I'd overheard...

Not flexible enough, I'm afraid.

No, definitely not.

And *I'd* thought they'd been talking about

me. But they must have been talking about the production.

"...Poppy Vernon."

Oh dear, I'd been in my own little world and now Tara was saying my name and I hadn't a clue why. I looked at Jasmine for help but she just hugged me and said, "Oh Poppy! That's totally brilliant!"

"Don't look so shocked, Poppy!" said Tara. "We've chosen you to be our dancing princess because of the wonderful expressive quality of your dance."

I couldn't take it in. I was going to burst into tears. No I wasn't, I was going to burst out laughing. No I wasn't. If only Tara would say it one more time so I could be completely sure she really did mean me... But it was Miss Coralie who spoke next.

"Congratulations, Poppy! You deserve it."

"Thank...you..." I said. "Oh...thank you."

10 A Touch of Magic

"Mrs. Vernon?" Tara suddenly said, looking over to the door.

And when I turned round, there was Mum hovering in the doorway. She nodded at Tara, but her eyes were asking a question at the same time.

"I've just told Poppy the good news," said Tara.

Mum broke into a smile and came to give me a hug.

"Did you know already?" I asked her.

"No, because Tara hadn't fully decided, but

she needed to check with me and Dad that we were happy to let you do all the rehearsals if you *did* get picked."

My body tingled with excitement and happiness as everyone came up to me and said, *Well done!* or *Congratulations!* Well, everyone except Tamsyn. She was standing with Lottie and Immy by the *barre*.

"It's only an amateur production, you know," she said loudly, wrinkling her nose. "I wouldn't want to dance unless it was a professional company. Would you?"

Lottie and Immy looked embarrassed and glanced over to check that Tara hadn't heard, but luckily she was talking to Miss Coralie at that moment.

"I'm so sorry Denis couldn't make it today. He's tied up with Chris Delaney."

"Chris Delaney!" squeaked Lottie. "He's famous!"

Everyone stopped talking and listened to

Tara. "Yes, we're very lucky to have Chris as our prince."

There were lots of gasps, and the tingles started charging round my body.

"I saw him on television last night!" said Sophie. "Oh wow, Poppy, you're going to meet Chris Delaney!"

Then Rose rushed in and gave me a hug. "You brilliant, clever thing, Poppy!"

"What are you doing still here?" I asked her.

"Mum said I could sit in the changing room during your class because I was so desperate to see who'd been chosen," she said. Then she gave me another hug. "Can you get me Chris Delaney's autograph?"

"If Poppy's appearing in the first half of the panto, I don't expect she'll get to see Chris Delaney all that much, will she?" Tamsyn asked Tara.

"Oh, I think she will." Tara smiled.

Jasmine gave me a big smile and I knew she

was thinking, *Good. Serves Tamsyn right.*

"Right, do you three want to get changed?" said Mum. "Then I can get you home." She turned to me. "I've invited Jasmine and Rose for tea."

What a perfect end to a perfectly perfect day! I started to go out to the changing room, but Rose called me back and when I turned she was standing there with her hands on her waist, looking like a strict mother. "And maybe now you'll believe me, Poppy Vernon, when I say that you can do *devil pays* better than I can!"

"*Développés!*" about six people corrected her.

"But I can't," I insisted. "You can make your leg go much higher than mine."

Rose did a big sigh. "How many times have I told you, you've got something else that makes it so good."

"Is it her shoulders?" asked Jasmine.

Rose shook her head.

"Her arms?" asked Lottie.

Rose shook her head again.

"Her back?" Sophie tried.

I'd completely forgotten that the grown-ups were still there, waiting for us to go, until Tara suddenly interrupted. "What Poppy has got," she said slowly and clearly, "is a touch of magic. An indescribable touch of magic." And Miss Coralie nodded, too, with proud eyes, looking right into mine.

And as Mum smiled at me across the room I really felt that magic. It fizzled and spun round inside me, like a sparkling wand, turning me into the happiest, happiest dancing princess in the whole wide world.

Basic Ballet Positions

First position

Second position

Third position

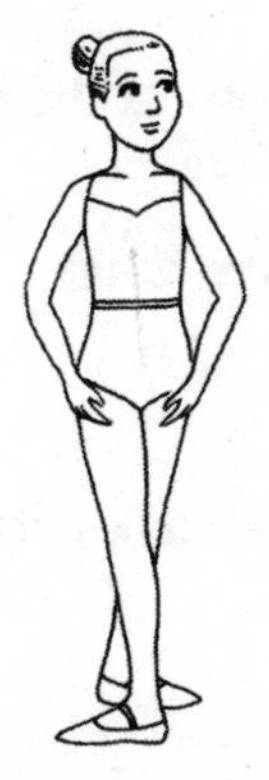

Fourth position

Fifth position

Ballet words are mostly in French, which makes them more magical. But when you're learning, it's nice to know what they mean too. Here are some of the words that all Miss Coralie's students have to learn:

adage The name for the slow steps in the centre of the room, away from the *barre.*

arabesque A beautiful balance on one leg.

assemblé A jump where the feet come together at the end.

battement dégagé A foot exercise at the *barre to* get beautiful toes.

battement tendu Another foot exercise where you stretch your foot until it points.

chassé A soft smooth slide of the feet.

développé A lifting and unfolding of one leg into the air, while balancing on the other.

fifth position croisé When you are facing, say the *left* corner, with your feet in fifth position, and your front foot is the *right* foot.

fouetté This step is so fast your feet are in a blur! You do it to prepare for *pirouettes.*

grand battement High kick!

jeté A spring where you land on the opposite foot. Rose loves these!

pas de bourrée Tiny little steps to the side, like a mouse.

pas de chat A cat hop from one foot to the other.

plié This is the first step we do in class. You have to bend your knees slowly and make sure your feet are turned right out, with your heels firmly planted on the floor for as long as possible.

port de bras Arm movements, which Poppy is good at.

révérence The curtsey at the end of class.

rond de jambe This is where you make a circle with your leg.

sissonne A scissor step.

sissonne en arrière A scissor step going backwards. This is really hard!

sissonne en avant A scissor step going forwards.

soubresaut A jump off two feet, pointing your feet hard in the air.

temps levé A step and sweep up the other leg then jump.

turnout You have to stand with your legs and feet and hips all opened out and pointing to the side, not the front. This is the most important thing in ballet that everyone learns right from the start.

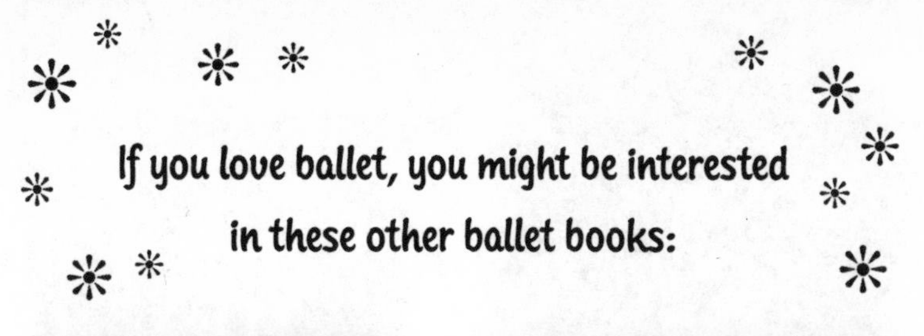

If you love ballet, you might be interested in these other ballet books:

ISBN PB 0 7460 5593 5
HB 0 7460 5594 3

ISBN 0 7460 1692 1

ISBN 0 7460 5899 3